AF482155

LAURA'S CHALLENGES

Ilustrated by

Clarissa Ricci

To my dear daughter, Aya.

May your childhood be

filled with joyful and happy

moments full of love and

sincere connections. I love

you! Mamae

This story is about a sweet and curious little girl named Laura, who was five years old when her parents decided they would no longer live together. At first, she felt a little confused, sad, and scared.

Laura clutched her teddy bear, Lico, and asked herself many questions, feeling utterly confused and full of doubt.

— How will my life be now? Will I still be able to see my friends? Will I continue going to the same school? When will I be able to be with Mom and Dad? And with my cousins from Brazil and my cousins who live in the United States? Where will my toys be? What will I do when I miss someone? Can I call people?

These thoughts caused a little ache in her stomach and made her anxious. She imagined herself alone, walking from one place to another without knowing what to expect. This feeling made her chest tighten, and she wished to stay still for a moment.

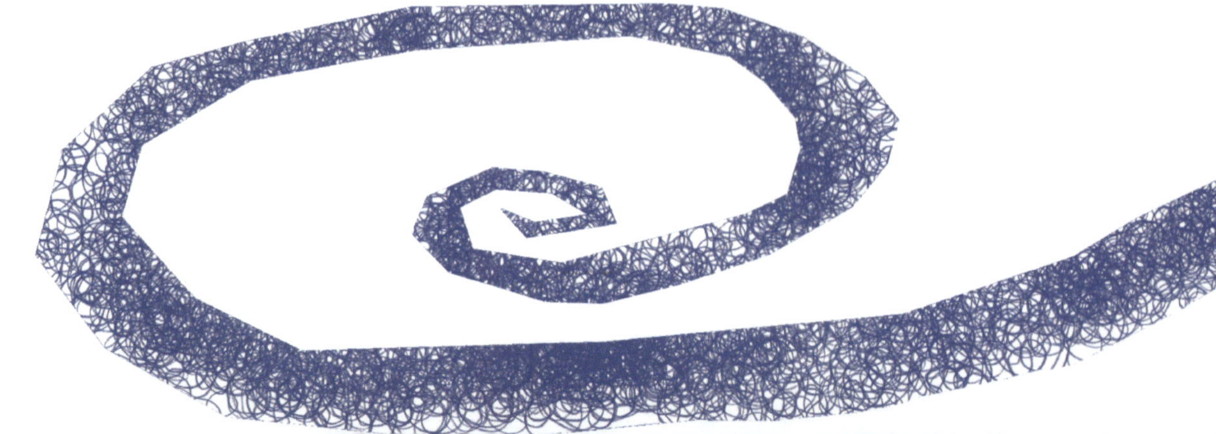

Laura was afraid that her parents might not want
to be friends anymore or that they would not like
each other, and worse...
She feared that they might stop liking her or
become upset with her!
She felt a chill in her stomach and wanted to hide.

— Dear teddy bear, my parents told me that even though they will live in separate houses, they'll always be close to me. They also said that I will always be the love of their lives!

8

Then, she realized that her time would be divided between two houses, in two different places.
In the United States, in the city where Laura was born and lived for most of her life, she would continue attending a beautiful school where people spoke English and Spanish. There, she learned to communicate in both languages with her friends.

She remembered the sandwiches and tasty fruits her mother packed in her lunch box with great care. She also recalled returning from school, whereupon her mom always welcomed her with repeated twirls in the air, hugs, kisses, and the most delightful scents.

— Lico, I'll take you to the park, and we'll go on all the rides! They're fun; you won't be scared!

Laura often received visits from her grandparents, uncles, and cousins. Additionally, she had close friends who were always with her.

Laura's parents also told her that she could spend her vacations with her grandparents, uncles, and cousins where her father had been born. There, she would experience different customs — riding motorcycles and bicycles, playing in the snow, visiting a beautiful lake, and ice skating. Laura loved these adventure-filled moments with her dad's family.

— Lico, every year, I will also spend time with my
godparents, other relatives, and cousins in Brazil.
They are so lively and funny! — Besides English
and Spanish, I speak and understand Portuguese!
In Brazil, we dance a lot, eat delicious cheese balls
"pão de queijo" and a kind of chocolate truffle
called "brigadeiro", which I love, and spend hours
at the beach, surfing the ocean waves.

Laura felt enveloped by all this love and energy.
Despite feeling sad and insecure about so many
changes, she faced this challenge with courage.
She would continue to be an affectionate,
strong, and joyful little girl, and her parents loved
her exactly the way she was.
Laura was no longer afraid!!!

Laura's parents always made sure to remind her that it was not her fault that they no longer lived together. Sometimes, adults make decisions to find more happiness, and even though they were separated, they would always be there to take care of her with all the love in the world.

Over time, Laura realized that the changes in
her life brought her great experiences. She had
the opportunity to immerse herself in different
cultures, travel to other places, and learn other
languages. She was certain that her family's love
would accompany her wherever she went, and
create an eternal bond between them.

So, Laura continued her journey through life, with a heart full of confidence due to all the experiences that made her feel she was a unique and loved person. She understood that, despite the changes, her parents' love connected her emotionally to both, no matter where she was.

Guided by this love, Laura felt she was ready to face all the difficulties that life had in store for her with joy and courage. Laura then understood the feeling of gratitude. She realized how thankful she was to everyone who was helping her throughout all the changes with kind and accepting words.

She remembered that there would be fun toys at both Mom's and Dad's houses. Her teddy bear Lico would always accompany her. Now, she felt light and confident, and she smiled.
Laura had a connection with all the people who cared about her and thought of them with great affection. There was a magical thread linking her heart to Mom's and Dad's hearts. And Laura was that magical thread!
She knew they would always be in her life to support her if she needed them.
She was calm and breathed deeply.

DO YOU KNOW WHICH GAMES LAURA LIKES THE MOST?

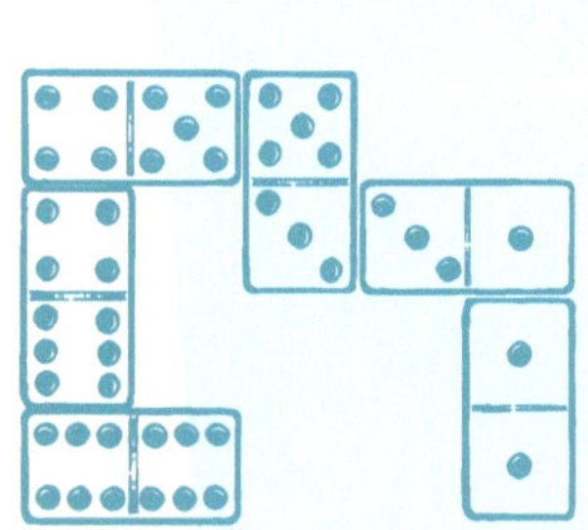

She likes to

- ride a bike,
- ride in a little car,
- play ball,
- play hide-and-seek,
- jump on the trampoline,
- play blindfolded games,
- build a sandcastle,
- play memory games,
- make "brigadeiro" balls,
- play bingo,
- pretend to cook for her dolls,
- take her little animals for a walk,
- draw and paint,
- jump rope,
- play dominoes!

— Why was Laura sad?

— What was Laura's biggest fear?

— What is her teddy bear's name?

— Where could she spend her vacation?

— Why did Laura finally calm down?

THE AUTHOR

MAIRA HORTA is a Brazilian licensed clinical therapist based in California, United States. Besides being the mother of a smart and playful little girl, she specializes in helping people overcome anxiety and trauma with a focus on cultural minorities. Part of her work is dedicated to empowering parents to raise conscious, loved, and confident children, even in situations of separation.

With her professional and personal experience, Maira understands the importance of helping families rise to challenges of cultural changes and face the pressures of modern life. She values the richness of cultural diversity and works to promote healthy emotional and psychological education for children growing up in multicultural environments.

Her goal is to provide tools and knowledge for parents to create a welcoming, safe, and loving environment for their children, thus allowing them to feel connected to their cultural roots while adapting to the diverse communities where they reside. She believes this is the best gift parents can give to their children — providing them with a solid foundation to face life's challenges with confidence and resilience.

The author is passionate about her work and is dedicated to helping individuals and families build strong and loving bonds, to promote healthy emotional and psychological development for their children.

Her writings and guidance draw on her professional experience, combining expertise in psychology with an understanding of the importance of maintaining a cultural identity in a diverse world.

THE ILLUSTRATOR

CLARISSA RICCI is an illustrator based in Brazil. She was born and raised in São Paulo, although living as well in fantastic realities through reading books and drawing for most of the time. She is fascinated by creating characters and worlds, lives which inhabit and populate several sketchbooks. Bachelor in Visual Arts from the Institute of Arts of São Paulo's State University (Unesp), she works as an illustrator and graphic designer since 2016, having worked as well as an art educator in cultural institutions such as SESC and the Museum of Modern Arts of São Paulo.

International Cataloging Data in Publication (CIP) according ISBD

H821l   Horta, Maira.
        Laura's challenges / Maira Horta ; illustrated by Clarissa Ricci. - Atibaia
: Author's edition, 2024
        32 p. ; 20,5cm x 27,5cm.

        ISBN: 978-65-982911-1-2

        1. Children's literature. 2. Family. 3. Cultural diversity. I. Ricci, Clarissa.
II. Título.

                                              CDD 028.5
2024-707   CDU 82-93
Index for systematic catalog:
Children's literature 028.5
Children's literature 82-93

Prepared by Vagner Rodolfo da Silva - CRB-8/9410